On and on, towards the stairs.
Would he dare to race down there?
Of course he would – he wasn't scared...
Be careful, fastest toy!

But Duck found out that stairs are steep,
not meant for wheels, but made for feet.
Clicketty, clacketty, rattle bang thump.
Daredevil Duck fell... with a

B
U M
P
!

Duck was broken, Duck had crashed,
his wheels could not be mended.
His head was chipped, his beak was bashed,
his racing days had ended.

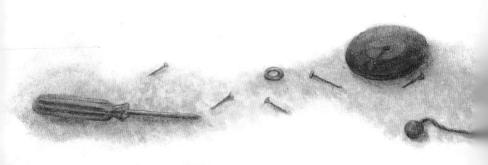

Duck missed the fun, after his fall.
He couldn't race, he could only crawl,
and he missed his old friends most of all,
now he wasn't the fastest toy.

But look! His racing days are back.
He's waving a flag at the end of the track.
When the winner comes by
        it's "QUACK QUACK QUACK!
Three cheers for the fastest toy."

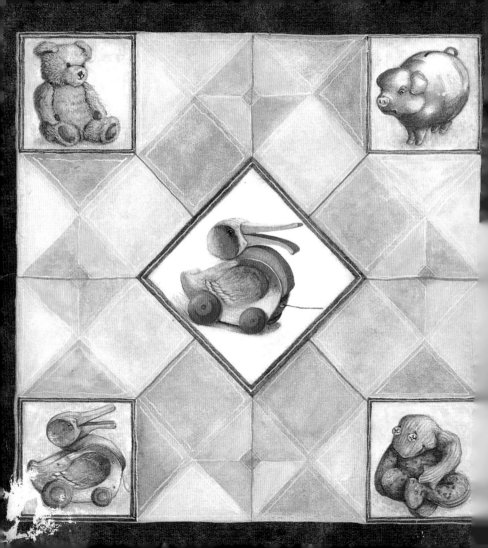